Buffalo Hunt

by Jay Carter

illustrated by John Martin

HOUGHTON MIFFLIN HARCOURT
School Publishers

PHOTOGRAPHY CREDITS: Cover (bkgd) Digital Vision/Getty Images. 18 © LMR Group/Alamy.

Printed in China

ISBN-10: 0-547-25322-2
ISBN-13: 978-0-547-25322-0

14 15 16 17 0940 19 18 17 16
4500569761

Learning to Hunt

Sean Nesbitt crawled along the pebbly bank of Nebraska's Platte River. This was amazing for several reasons. First, until a few months ago, the 16-year-old had been living with his family in New York City, a great distance from Nebraska. Second, Sean was carrying a bow and arrow. And finally, he was crawling through the dirt next to his new friend, a Pawnee teenager named Sharp Eyes.

And to think that all this is happening in 1867, thought Sean. He couldn't help chuckling out loud at how crazy it all seemed. Sharp Eyes shot him a critical look and raised his finger to his lips.

The young Pawnee was teaching Sean to hunt, and the first rule of hunting was absolute quiet. If your prey heard you coming, you'd be having beans for supper instead of meat. Sean immediately went silent and focused on the task at hand.

They had been stalking a jackrabbit all morning. It was taking all morning because every time they got near enough to fire an arrow, Sean would cough or kick a rock. Or he'd make some other noise that would give them away, and the rabbit would bolt for cover. Sean would get angry with himself. But Sharp Eyes would just wait patiently, explain how Sean could avoid repeating his mistake, and take off after the rabbit again.

Sean felt envy for Sharp Eyes's hunting skills and knowledge. The Pawnee boy knew how to stay downwind of their quarry so the animal couldn't smell them. And he was able to move quickly and purposefully without making a sound.

Sean was astonished at the way his friend tracked animals silently through the brush. Sharp Eyes could catch a quail in a snare and follow an elk trail across a river. Sean wanted to learn everything he could about hunting in the little time he would have with Sharp Eyes. Sean and his father were part of the crew that was building the Union Pacific Railroad, and they would soon be moving to a new location.

Sharp Eyes pointed. Sean could just make out the rabbit, camouflaged against the branches and leaves of a bush. Quietly, Sean fitted an arrow to his bow, took aim, and let it fly.

The jackrabbit leapt into the air and took off running, uninjured. It didn't get far. Sean missed, but Sharp Eyes didn't. The rabbit fell dead, a feathered arrow protruding from its side… a perfect shot.

Later, the boys were enjoying fresh-roasted rabbit in front of a small fire in Sharp Eyes's village. Sharp Eyes paused to thank the rabbit for its sacrifice before they dug into the hot and greasy meal. It tasted wonderful, especially after all the hard work that had gone into getting it.

Sean warmed his hands over the fire. At first he had
been shocked by the idea of using dried buffalo dung to
build a fire. But on the western plains, there were very few
trees to cut down for fuel.

Wiping his chin, Sean considered the rows of earthen
lodges and the Pawnee men and women going about their
business. It was like a scene from the Western adventure
magazines he loved to read. But actually being there made
it all seem so normal. As he got to know the people in the
Pawnee village, their hopes and desires seemed to him to
have much in common with those of the people he knew
back in the East.

Sean's Story

While they were hunting, Sharp Eyes was the teacher and Sean the student. But after the hunt, it was Sean's turn to answer questions.

Sean's family had immigrated to America from Ireland. Mr. Nesbitt had had difficulty finding work in New York City, so he had taken a job cooking for the crews building the railroad that would span the continent. Sean's mother and sister had stayed behind in the care of Mr. Nesbitt's older brother and his family. But Mr. Nesbitt had asked Sean to come with him. Sean would be a big help, and he thought the boy could do with a bit of adventure.

Sharp Eyes wanted to find out everything he could about Sean and his world. He quizzed him about Ireland. "This Saint Pat-uh-rick had medicine to banish snakes? That is powerful medicine." He marveled at Sean's ocean journey. "You saw no land... for days? The ocean sounds like the prairie with water instead of grass." He asked about New York. "If no one hunts, what do you eat?"

But mostly, Sharp Eyes asked about the railroad. He was fascinated by the metal rails that stretched as far as the eye could see.

Pawnee warriors were providing security for the railroad crews. The farther the tracks pushed into the frontier, the more danger the crews faced from hostile nations like the Sioux and Cheyenne. These nations, especially, wanted to halt the building of the railroad because they felt that the white people brought nothing but sorrow to the nations.

As part of their payment, the Pawnee could ride the trains for free. Sharp Eyes hoped to travel one day to the faraway places that those rails would lead to—the busy coastal cities, the oceans on either side of the continent. He asked so many questions because he wanted to be prepared for whatever he found when he got there.

Sean's Request

Sean finished explaining what an elevator was. As the conversation lulled, he got up his nerve. Sean had been wanting to ask a favor and decided to ask now before his courage deserted him.

"Sharp Eyes, if your people hunt buffalo soon," he began, "may I come with you?"

The Pawnee considered the question. "Don't your people go hunting?"

"Some men went the other day. But they said I was too young."

Sharp Eyes thought for a long time. Finally, he pulled himself upright and replied, "You are not too young. But no one outside the nation has ever come before. I will have to ask the shaman."

"What is a shaman?"

"A wise man in our nation." Sharp Eyes added, "Sometimes we have to ride for many days to find a herd."

"I don't mind," Sean shot back. "And I know my father would let me go."

"It can be very dangerous," warned Sharp Eyes.

"I'll be careful and stay out of everyone's way," promised Sean eagerly. "I just want to see a hunt."

Sharp Eyes thought again. A dog passing by tried to steal a bite of Sean's rabbit. Sharp Eyes shooed it off with a stone. The dog bared its teeth but ran off.

"I will ask," he said, finally breaking into a smile. "But you have a lot of practicing to do. Hunting buffalo is a lot harder than hunting jackrabbits."

The next afternoon, when Sean had finished his chores and ran to find his friend, Sharp Eyes wasn't smiling. He stood on the margins of the railroad camp holding two ponies. Sean couldn't clearly read his friend's expression. He thought Sharp Eyes looked sad, angry, confused.

"What's wrong?" Sean asked, worried.

But all the Pawnee boy said was, "Come."

A Terrible Slaughter

Sean and Sharp Eyes rode for an hour before they came to the spot. At first Sean didn't understand why his friend had brought him here. But then he saw. Twenty buffalo were lying dead on the prairie. A few had been partially skinned, and a little meat had been taken. But mostly, they had been killed needlessly and left to rot in the sun.

"Your people did this," said Sharp Eyes. "They shot the buffalo and laughed. And then… they just… went away. Why?"

Sean realized the question was directed to him.

"Why?" Sharp Eyes repeated.

"Why would anyone do this? Take lives for nothing?" Sharp Eyes was having trouble controlling his feelings.

Sean stood open-mouthed. He did not have an answer. Sharp Eyes's anger grew as he spoke. "These creatures are a gift from Tirawa, our god. The meat feeds us. The skins keep us warm in winter. The bones give us tools. The tendons make thread and bowstrings. I've seen how your people waste things in your camp... how they leave entire villages behind when your workers move down the line. But this..." He pointed at the rotting bodies. "This..." Words failed him.

Sean could only hang his head.

"Maybe the Sioux are right," said Sharp Eyes sadly as he collected himself. "Maybe it is a mistake to welcome your people. Your railroad will bring great things to our land. But I fear it will bring great sorrow, too."

Sharp Eyes mounted his horse and rode away.

Sean didn't see Sharp Eyes for days. He had plenty of time to think about his friend's question. Why had the men killed so cruelly and needlessly? The buffalo weren't dangerous. The railroad camp had plenty of meat. No matter how he reasoned, he didn't have an answer.

The Buffalo Hunt

One day the following week, Sean was awakened well before dawn by Sharp Eyes.

He stood by the entrance to Sean's tent. "Come," he said. But today he didn't look angry.

At the edge of the camp, Sharp Eyes spoke again. "A herd of buffalo has come. There will be a hunt. The shaman says that you will hunt with us."

Sean wanted to come, but his crew would be leaving later that day. He started to speak, but Sharp Eyes stopped him.

"We will be back in time. The shaman says that we must share our ways. If your people understand, perhaps they will not waste the buffalo. You shall be the one to tell them. Will you come?" Sharp Eyes smiled and held out the reins to a pony.

Sean did not hesitate. He smiled back and swung into the saddle. "You bet!" he replied.

The Pawnees had gathered near a herd of thousands and thousands of buffalo. In some places, the animals were packed so closely together that they looked like a forest of fur. Sharp Eyes told Sean that the village had been preparing for days, praying and dancing. After the shaman blessed the warriors, scouts dressed in wolf robes snuck up on the herd. Buffalo didn't fear wolves, and the braves knew that they wouldn't react if they caught the smell.

A string of warriors had ridden out in two directions to surround the herd. A few carried rifles. Most had bows and arrows. On a scout's signal, they charged. And Sean charged after them.

What followed was chaos. Dust flew as the buffalo stampeded. The wind carried the hunting cries of the Pawnee and the snorts and squeals of the animals. The warriors chased them, firing arrow after arrow. Sean saw how Sharp Eyes got his name. A large buffalo soon fell before his bow.

Sean did his best to keep up with the Pawnee, but it was soon clear that they outstripped him in skill and agility. When a massive bull nearly trampled Sean, he decided to head for cover. He was happy to let the more experienced hunters do their work.

Sean wasn't sure how long the hunt lasted. Ten minutes? Half an hour? But the action didn't stop until the animals that had been spared stampeded into the distance.

After the Hunt

But the hunt was nothing compared to what happened next. In a whirl of activity, the entire nation descended on the fallen animals. The buffalo skins were removed and rolled up to be taken back to the village, where they would be tanned and turned into tents, rugs, leather, robes, dresses, and pants. The meat was harvested. Some would be cooked; the remainder would be cut into strips to be dried. The bones would be used to make everything from garden hoes to children's toys.

As he watched, Sean was filled with awe and respect. He saw how everyone worked together and how nothing was wasted. No buffalo died without reason.

A Promise

The boys returned to the railroad camp a few hours later. The men were already packing up, getting ready to move to the next stop down the line.

"Tell your people. They must change their ways." There was no laughter in Sharp Eyes's voice as he urged Sean to convince his people.

The boys silently watched as the railroad men tossed trash onto an ever-growing pile.

"I'll tell them," vowed Sean.

Sharp Eyes looked at the tracks that disappeared into the distance. He seemed wistful.

"And," Sean continued, "I'll show 'em, too. I promise never to kill a buffalo, or any other animal, wastefully. If I set a good example, it may help them see."

Sharp Eyes nodded. "This could be powerful medicine."

Sean held out his hand. "Thank you, Sharp Eyes. You've taught me a lot."

Sharp Eyes grasped Sean's hand. Then, with a wave, he turned and walked away. Sean watched his friend disappear into the bright rays of the morning sun. Then Sean turned and headed toward the camp. He had a promise to keep.

Afterword

The mass slaughter of the buffalo on the Great Plains took place during the mid-1800s. Railroad passengers crossing the plains were encouraged to shoot the majestic creatures from moving trains for "sport"—just to watch them fall. That practice ended only because the smell of the rotting buffalo beside the tracks made passengers ill.

Buffalo fur became fashionable, and buffalo meat became a delicacy served in restaurants. Hoping to make a fortune from buffalo hides, pioneers killed the animals by the thousands. Hunters shot until they ran out of ammunition or until their gun barrels got too hot to hold. "Buffalo Bill" Cody, one of the greatest showmen of the Old West, is said to have killed several thousand buffalo in just a few months.

The slaughter of the buffalo had a major effect on the nations who inhabited the Great Plains. Nations such as the Pawnee, who depended on the buffalo, lost one of their most important food sources, as well as a significant part of their culture. Eventually, most nations were forced to move onto reservations set up by the U.S. government.

Millions of buffalo roamed the Great Plains when Europeans first arrived in North America. By 1885, the buffalo was nearly extinct in America, with only about 1,000 of the animals still living. Today, thanks to careful breeding, there are nearly 500,000 buffalo in preserves throughout the United States.

Responding

✔ **TARGET SKILL** **Theme** What do Sean's and Sharp Eyes's thoughts and actions tell you about the theme of the story? What text details support your conclusion? Copy and complete the chart below.

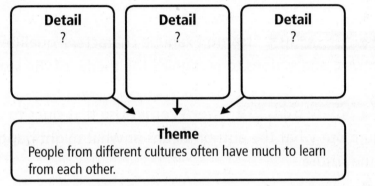

Detail	Detail	Detail
?	?	?

Theme
People from different cultures often have much to learn from each other.

Write About It

Text to Text Think of a story you have read about two friends like Sean and Sharp Eyes who come from different cultures. Write a few paragraphs comparing and contrasting Sean and Sharp Eyes with the characters you have chosen.

✔ **TARGET VOCABULARY**

astonished	margins
banish	nerve
bared	reasoned
deserted	spared
envy	upright

✔ **TARGET SKILL** **Theme** Examine characters' qualities, motives, and actions to recognize the theme of the story.

✔ **TARGET STRATEGY** **Infer/Predict** Use text clues to figure out what the author means or what might happen in the future.

GENRE Historical Fiction is a story whose characters and events are set in a real period of history.